KU-165-741

Railway Series, No. 14

THE LITTLE OLD ENGINE

by

THE REV. W. AWDRY

with illustrations by
JOHN T. KENNEY

HEINEMANN · LONDON

William Heinemann Ltd
Michelin House
81 Fulham Road
London SW3 6RB

LONDON MELBOURNE AUCKLAND

First published in 1959
Copyright © William Heinemann Ltd 1959
Reprinted 1990
All rights reserved

ISBN 0 434 92791 0

Printed and bound in Great Britain by
William Clowes Limited, Beccles and London

DEAR FRIENDS,

You remember in *Four Little Engines* that Sir Handel Brown, The Owner, sent Skarloey away to be mended. These stories tell what happened when the "Little Old Engine" came home.

Skarloey is not real. You can only see him in these books. *But there is a real engine just like Skarloey.* He is very, very old, and has been mended. His name is Talyllyn, and he lives at Towyn in Wales.

You would all enjoy going to see him at work.

THE AUTHOR

The author gratefully acknowledges the help given by fellow members of the Talyllyn Railway Preservation Society in the preparation of this book.

Trucks!

SIR HANDEL and Peter Sam had hard work while Skarloey was away. The Owner gave them buffers, and even bought a Diesel named Rusty; but Sir Handel grumbled continually.

One day Gordon saw him shunting, and laughed.

"My Controller *makes* me shunt," Sir Handel said sheepishly, "*and* take trucks to quarries too. I'm highly sprung, and I suffer dreadfully".

"Our Controllers don't understand our feelings," sympathised Gordon. "Now, if you were ill"—he winked—"you couldn't go, could you?"

"Good idea," said Sir Handel. "I'll try it."

"I don't feel well," he groaned next morning.

There wasn't time to examine him then, so some of the trucks were coupled behind Peter Sam's coaches, and Rusty promised to follow with the rest.

"He! He! He!" sniggered Sir Handel; but no one noticed. They were all too busy.

Peter Sam didn't mind the extra work. He left his coaches at the Top Station, and trundled cheerfully through the woods. The trucks chattered behind him in an agitated way, but he paid no attention.

It might have been better if he had.

Slates come from quarries high up in the hills. They travel down in trucks on a steep railway called an Incline. Empty trucks at the bottom are hitched to a rope. Loaded ones at the top are hitched to one another. By their weight, loaded trucks run down the Incline pulling up empty ones.

There are strong brakes in the Winding House at the top to prevent loaded trucks from running down too fast. The ropes are very strong too, but in spite of this, trucks sometimes play dangerous tricks.

Peter Sam never bumped trucks unless they misbehaved. Sir Handel bumped them even if they were good; so they didn't like him, and played tricks whenever they could.

Peter Sam pushed the empty trucks to a siding where his Fireman hitched them to the rope. Then, on another siding, he pulled back some loaded trucks. With these in front of him, he stood waiting.

More loaded trucks stood at the top of the Incline, ready to come down. They couldn't see Peter Sam. They thought he was Sir Handel, and wanted to pay him out.

They began to move. "Faster! Faster!" they grumbled. They reached halfway, gathering speed.

"Scrag him! Scrag him!" they yelled.

"No! No!" wailed the empty trucks. "It's Peter Sam! It's Peter Sam!" But it was no use. The loaded trucks were straining at the rope.

They broke it with a CRACK! "Hurrah! Hurrah!" they roared, hurtling down the hill.

Peter Sam heard them. He shut his eyes. His Driver and Fireman crouched in his cab.

The crash jerked him violently backwards.

"Ouch!" he shivered. "I didn't expect a cold bath."

The water poured from a channel smashed by flying slates. He was soaked from funnel to cab.

"Peep! Peep!" he spluttered, and was glad when he heard Rusty's answering "Toot!"

"Bust my buffers!" exclaimed Rusty. "What a mess! Never mind, Peter Sam, we'll get you out." He soon pulled him away from the water and the trucks.

Peter Sam felt battered. His funnel was cracked and his boiler dented, but he was glad his Driver and Fireman were unhurt.

He thanked Rusty, and limped slowly home. Rusty stayed to help clear the wreckage.

"I'm sorry about your accident, Peter Sam," said Sir Handel. "I always stand well back. Trucks don't like me, you see."

"Why didn't you warn me?"

"I didn't think . . ."

"You never do," said a stern voice. "You can start now while you are doing Peter Sam's work as well as your own. That'll teach you to pretend you are ill."

Sir Handel did start thinking. He thought about Thin Controllers, and he thought about Gordon. He wanted to give Gordon a piece of his mind!

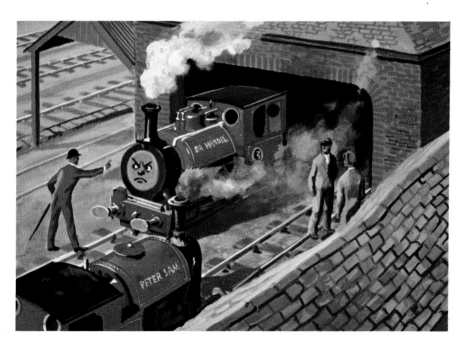

Home at Last

PETER SAM wanted to start work; but the Thin Controller wouldn't let him. "Another day's rest will do you good," he said. "Besides, I've got a surprise for you."

"For me Sir! How nice Sir! What is it Sir?"

"Wait and see," smiled the Thin Controller. The "Surprise" was Skarloey. "Oh!" said Peter Sam, "I am glad you've come home."

They lit Skarloey's fire, and he sizzled happily. "I feel all excited," he said, "just like a young engine. I'm longing to pull my dear old coaches again. Are they running nicely?"

"Yes, they're running well," Peter Sam answered, "but we have five other coaches now."

Skarloey was interested. "Oh!" he said, "tell me about them."

"Cora is a Guard's Van. She isn't as big as Beatrice, and she hasn't a Ticket Window, but I like her best. She was my Guard's Van in the old days. Ada, Jane and Mabel are plain. They have no roofs. Sir Handel says they are trucks; but they have seats," said Peter Sam, "so *I* say they're coaches. What do you think, Skarloey?"

The old engine smiled. "If they have seats, they're coaches," he said firmly.

"Sir Handel likes Gertrude and Millicent best," Peter Sam went on. "He always tries to take them alone. They have bogies, and he says they're the only real coaches we have. They remind him of when he used to pull our Express. Both have seats for passengers, but Millicent has a Guard as well. He sells tickets and travels in a tiny cupboard place.

"I don't like that," he remarked earnestly. "Guards are very important. They need Vans. They shouldn't be put into cupboards."

Skarloey said nothing, so Peter Sam continued.

"Did Rusty help you off your truck?"

"Yes, he says he's come to mend the line and do odd jobs. I like him," smiled Skarloey.

"So do I." Peter Sam explained how kind Rusty was when he had his accident. "It's a pity Duncan doesn't like him."

"Who is Duncan?"

"He came as a spare engine after my accident."

"Is he Useful?"

"He'll pull anything, and I'm sure he means well: but he's bouncy and rude. He used to work in a factory, and his language is often strong."

"I understand," said Skarloey gravely.

Just then the telephone rang, and Skarloey's Driver and Fireman climbed into his cab.

"Come on, Old Boy," they said, "Duncan is stuck in the tunnel, and we'll have to get him out."

Skarloey was pleased. He wanted a run, and looked forward to meeting Duncan.

They found Cora and some workmen, and hurried up the line.

"How nice and smooth the rails are!" thought Skarloey. "They've mended all the old bumps. Rusty has helped to do that. I must tell him how nice it is."

Duncan had stuck at the far end of the tunnel. His coaches were outside, and the passengers were helping the Driver and Fireman to dislodge some rocks wedged between the top of his cab and the tunnel roof.

Duncan was cross. "I'm a plain blunt engine," he kept saying, "I speak as I find. Tunnels should be tunnels, and not rabbit holes. This Railway is no good at all."

"Don't be silly," snapped his Driver. "This tunnel is quite big enough for engines who don't want to Rock 'n' Roll."

They cleared away the rocks, and Skarloey pulled Duncan and his coaches safely through. Cora was left on a siding, and the workmen stayed to make sure all was safe.

Duncan grumbled all the way home, but Skarloey paid no attention.

The Thin Controller was waiting for them.

"Listen to me, Duncan," he said, "there is nothing wrong with that tunnel. You stuck because you tried to do Rock 'n' Roll. If it happens again, I'll cut down your cab, and your funnel too."

Duncan, abashed, was neither plain nor blunt for a whole evening.

Rock 'n' Roll

WHEN Skarloey's turn came, he was glad to take out the coaches and meet old friends. He met Rusty up the line. "You know," he said, "if I couldn't see the old places, I'd think I was on a different railway."

Rusty laughed. "We hoped you would. Mr Hugh, our Foreman, said 'Rusty, Skarloey's coming home. Let's mend the track so well that he won't know where he is!' And we did, and you didn't; if you take my meaning."

Skarloey chuckled away. He liked this hard-working, friendly little engine.

"There's still one bad bit," said Rusty anxiously that evening. "It's just before the first station. We hadn't time."

"Never mind!" said Skarloey. "It's much better now than it was."

"Maybe better; but it's not good," replied Rusty. "An engine might come off there. Peter Sam and Sir Handel take care, and so do you, but I'm worried about Duncan. He *will* do Rock 'n' Roll. I shouldn't like his passengers hurt."

"What's that about me? I'm a plain engine and believe in plain speaking. Speak up, and stop whispering in corners."

Rusty told Duncan about the bad bit of line, and warned him to be careful.

"Huh!" he grunted, "I know my way about, thank you! *I* don't need smelly Diesels to tell me what to do."

Rusty looked hurt.

"Never mind," said Skarloey, "you've done your best." He said no more, but he thought a great deal.

Next morning Rusty left Duncan to find his own coaches. Duncan snorted and banged about the Yard, then clattered crossly to the station.

James was there already. "You're late," he snapped.

"I know," said Duncan, "it's that smelly Diesel's fault. He thinks he can teach me how to stay on the rails, and then goes off and leaves me to find my own coaches."

"You poor engine," sympathised James. "I know all about Diesels. One crept into our Yard, and ordered us about. *I* soon sent him packing."

Duncan gazed at him admiringly. He didn't know that James was boastful, and sometimes didn't tell the truth.

"Send him packing! Send him packing!" snorted Duncan. He climbed the first hill furiously.

"Well done, boy! Keep it up!" encouraged his Driver.

They were soon near the first station.

Duncan was pleased. "Nothing's happened! Nothing's happened!" he chortled. "Silly old Diesel! Clever me!" and he swaggered along doing his Rock 'n' Roll.

"Steady, boy!" his Driver tried to check him, but too late.

There was a tearing, cracking, crunching sound, and Duncan stopped bumpily.

"Sleepers and ballast!" he exclaimed. "I'm off!" And he was!

"I warned him," said Rusty crossly. "'Duncan,' I said, 'you be careful on that bit of line'; but all he did was to call me names."

Mr Hugh kept turning Rusty's handle. "Come on!" he urged. "Start up."

"No, Mr Hugh Sir, I'm sorry to disoblige, but I *won't* help that Duncan."

"I'm ashamed of you, Rusty," said Skarloey severely, "think of the passengers. What are they going to do?"

"Oh!" said Rusty, "I'd forgotten them. I'm sorry, Mr Hugh Sir. We must help the passengers," and his engine roared into life.

"Oh dear!" thought Duncan, "now everyone will know how silly I am."

Presently Mr Hugh and Rusty brought sleepers and old rails. Mr Hugh showed the passengers how to use them, and they soon levered Duncan back to the line.

Duncan was extra careful all day.

"Rusty," he whispered that night, "thank you for helping. I'm sorry I was rude."

"That's all right."

"I wish all Diesels were like you. Let's be friends."

"Suits me," smiled Rusty. "We'll mend that bad bit first thing tomorrow."

Little Old Twins

ONE day the Owner brought some people to see the Railway. He showed them everything. They travelled in the trains, and looked at stations, and bridges, and coaches.

"Yes," they would say thoughtfully, "we'll take this"; or "No, we won't take that."

They made notes in their books.

Peter Sam whispered to Sir Handel. "Men came and did that on our old line."

"And then," said Sir Handel, "soon afterwards, it was . . . it was . . ."

"Sold," finished Peter Sam mournfully.

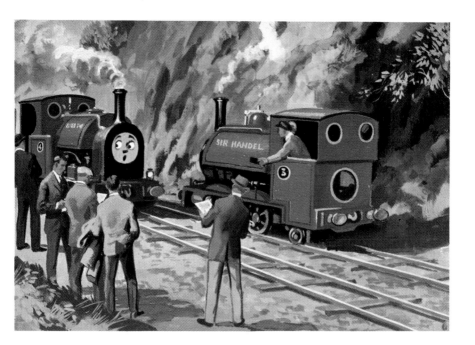

Peter Sam didn't sing any more. He wanted to cry. The other engines were sad too.

"What's the matter with you all?" his Driver asked him one day. "You look like dying ducks!"

"We don't want to be sold," said Peter Sam miserably.

"Sold!" the Driver was surprised. "Who to?"

"To those people who came and talked about taking things."

"You silly little engine," laughed his Driver. "They're not going to buy us. They're going to take our pictures on Television." And he tried to explain what that meant.

"Not going to be sold! Not going to be sold!" sang Peter Sam. He could hardly wait to tell the others. He told them about the Television as well, and they were pleased and excited too—all except Sir Handel.

"I don't hold with it," he grumbled. "Vulgar, I call it. Fancy traipsing about making an exhibition of yourselves. I won't do it, I tell you. Tellysomething indeed! Just let the Thin Controller come here, I'll tell him something!"

Skarloey said nothing. He just winked at Peter Sam—like this.

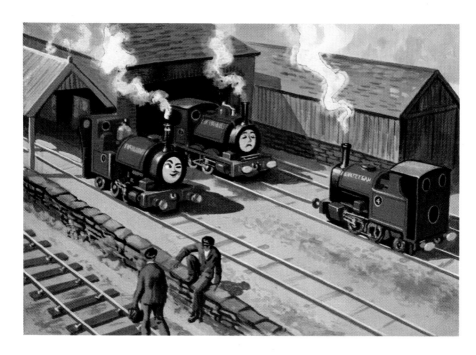

But next day, when the Thin Controller did come to explain about the Television, Sir Handel kept strangely quiet!

"Now," said the Thin Controller at last, "I want every engine to take part."

"I d-d-don't feel well," quavered Sir Handel.

"You poor engine," said the Thin Controller gravely, "you can stay in the Shed . . ."

Sir Handel smiled broadly!

". . . and your Driver and Fireman shall take you to pieces. That will make a very interesting picture. Just what we need."

Sir Handel's feelings were beyond words!

"That's that," said the Thin Controller.

"Now Skarloey, will you take Agnes, Ruth, Lucy, Jemima and Beatrice?"

"Yes please Sir. I was hoping you would let me have them."

"Duncan shall have a goods train, while Rusty, with Mr Hugh and the men, can show how we mend the line."

"Please Sir! What about me Sir?" asked Peter Sam anxiously.

The Thin Controller smiled. "You, Peter Sam, shall pull the special Television train."

"Oh Sir! Oh Sir!" bubbled Peter Sam in ecstasy.

The Television men built towers for cameras beside the line. They put cameras on Ada too, and filled Gertrude with wires and instruments. Some trucks, coupled behind, carried aerials and generators.

Everyone practised hard till they knew just what they had to do.

At last the time came, and the Announcer gave the signal. "We're on the air! We're on the air!" puffed Peter Sam, and he rolled the heavy train to the "Shops", where Sir Handel was being mended.

Sir Handel did *not* enjoy their visit!

"We're on the air! We're on the air," chanted Peter Sam. He trundled over the bridge near the middle station. "Peep Peep!" he whistled to Duncan, "we're coming!"

The Announcer talked to Duncan, and then they puffed over the second bridge to Quarry Siding, where Rusty, Mr Hugh and the men were waiting to explain about their work.

Soon they had to go. Peter Sam whistled, Rusty tooted in reply, and they clattered through the tunnel, rumbled over the viaduct near the waterfall, and rolled at last into the Top Station.

The Owner climbed down. "We arranged for Television," he said, "to let everyone see our Little Old Engine. We are proud of him, 95 years old and good as new! There's nothing like him anywhere. Three cheers for Skarloey."

"Peep! Peep! Peep!" whistled Peter Sam, and everybody joined in.

Skarloey smiled. "I'm very glad to be home again. Thank you Sir, and all, for your nice surprise. Now I'll surprise you. Listen! When I was mended in England, I found my Twin!"

The Owner stared. "Is there really another engine like you?"

"Yes Sir," chuckled Skarloey, "there is. Another engine came to be mended too, called Talyllyn. When the workmen saw us together, they laughed and called us their 'little old twins'.

"Talyllyn told me about his Railway. It is a lovely one, at Towyn in Wales.

"Well Sir, they mended us both and sent us home; but I often think of Talyllyn. He's 95 years old too, just like me.

"Please go to see him, all of you, and wish him 'Dry rails and good running' from Skarloey, his 'Little Old Twin'. "

We are indebted to John Adams (Publicity) Ltd for help in the preparation of the picture opposite